For Chesney —E.B.

BLOOMSBURY CHILDREN'S BOOKS
Bloomsbury Publishing Inc., part of Bloomsbury Publishing Plc
1385 Broadway, New York, NY 10018

BLOOMSBURY, BLOOMSBURY CHILDREN'S BOOKS, and the Diana logo are
trademarks of Bloomsbury Publishing Plc

First published in the United States of America in February 2022
by Bloomsbury Children's Books

Bloomsbury books may be purchased for business or promotional use.
For information on bulk purchases please contact Macmillan Corporate and
Premium Sales Department at specialmarkets@macmillan.com

Library of Congress Cataloging-in-Publication Data
Names: Brown, Elizabeth, author. | Stadtlander, Becca, illustrator.
Title: Like a diamond in the sky : Jane Taylor's beloved poem of wonder and the stars /
by Elizabeth Brown ; illustrated by Becca Stadtlander.
Description: New York : Bloomsbury, 2022. | Includes bibliographical references.
Summary: This picture book biography shines a light on the little-known poet and author of the
beloved lullaby and tells the story behind the classic and universally recognized rhyme.
Identifiers: LCCN 2021026265 (print) | LCCN 2021026266 (e-book)
ISBN 978-1-5476-0427-2 (hardcover) • ISBN 978-1-5476-0428-9 (e-book)
ISBN 978-1-5476-0429-6 (e-PDF)
Subjects: LCSH: Taylor, Jane, 1783–1824—Juvenile literature. | Taylor, Jane, 1783–1824. Twinkle,
twinkle, little star—Juvenile literature. | Authors, English—19th century—Biography—
Juvenile literature. | LCGFT: Biography. | Picture books.
Classification: LCC PR5549.T2 Z55 2022 (print) | LCC PR5549.T2 (e-book) | DDC 821/.7 [B]—dc23
LC record available at https://lccn.loc.gov/2021026265
LC e-book record available at https://lccn.loc.gov/2021026266

Artwork for this book was hand painted with gouache.
Typeset in Palatino LT Std.
Book design by Jeanette Levy
Printed in China by Leo Paper Products, Heshan, Guangdong
2 4 6 8 10 9 7 5 3 1

To find out more about our authors and books visit
www.bloomsbury.com and sign up for our newsletters.

LIKE A
DIAMOND
IN THE SKY

JANE TAYLOR'S BELOVED POEM
OF WONDER AND THE STARS

ELIZABETH BROWN
ILLUSTRATED BY BECCA STADTLANDER

BLOOMSBURY
CHILDREN'S BOOKS
NEW YORK LONDON OXFORD NEW DELHI SYDNEY

In the days when girls were taught to spin wool into yarn, set the table for tea, and smile and curtsy at the right times, Jane Taylor lived a different kind of childhood, schooled by nature and the stars.

Her parents took Jane and her sister, Ann, to the meadow to
count butterflies in the sun. They went on walks to study trees
and leaves. Each day, they spent time in their large garden creating
rhymes and couplets about the beauty of the countryside and the
flowers and animals that lived around them.

Jane's mother and her daughters sang
songs and hymns as they did their household
chores, and at night, the whispery hush of her
mother's soft singing soothed Jane to sleep.

Her father, an artist and a minister, taught Jane all about the stars.
The stories turned stars into fairy tales, their arrangements like
magic in the sky.

As she grew, Jane sought to contemplate
the dark blue depths of the sky,
to understand the mysteries of the night.
What makes stars sparkle and shine?

Jane thought she heard the words of a
poem as she looked toward the stars, and in the *hush hush*
of her mother's soft singing. Poetry and music swirled together in the
evening breeze, like a lullaby.

Jane wrote as fast as the words could flow from her quill, to share what
she felt when she gazed at the stars.

Jane wished for her words to sparkle and shine.

Jane's family lived in a cottage where books were read and cherished like friends. Her mother insisted the children take turns reading aloud during family meals. Whenever it was Jane's turn, she read poetry. Then the Taylors discussed each poem. Jane loved learning about

the flow of the words as she ate breakfast,

the art of the verses at midday lunch, and

the beauty of language during dinner.

Books were also a livelihood for the Taylor family. Each morning, Jane's father engraved art for books. He etched drawings and illustrations into copper plates, rolled on the ink, and pressed, making illustrations come alive on the page.

Jane practiced her writing by creating stories and poems from the finished art she saw. She recited her spirited rhymes seated upon the kneading board at the baker's shop, delighting customers buying cakes and bread, and she told her tales around farmer Blackadder's hearth at his annual country dance.

When Jane strolled across the moor with her sister, gathering bouquets of wildflowers at dusk, she discovered that poetry was all around her:

In the pattern of the seasons changing,
the lyric songs of skylarks and nightingales,
the crescendo and cadence of a river rushing,
and the rhythm of dawn to dusk.
Poems danced in her head.

Jane sewed together little books of her poems and gave them as gifts.

She wrote title pages and dedications to friends and family, preparing for when she would be a real poet.

Jane joined a writing group where she and her sister shared their poems with other young girls in hopes of someday publishing them.

Society called women writers *bluestockings*: women who read too much, knew too much, and wrote too much. People mocked any woman who believed learning and education were more important than the rules of proper English society, just like they would scorn a woman wearing blue woolen stockings instead of dainty white ones.

"Bluestocking! Women are to be seen, not heard."

Women were never supposed to shine too bright but be like distant flickering stars in the dark midnight sky.

"The spider is weaving her delicate thread, which brilliantly glitters with dew."

Jane worked in the family business, like most unmarried
women would in those days, to be safe, certain, and secure a
means to independence.

She etched, she inked, and she pressed,
engraving after engraving, plate after copper plate.

Jane enjoyed being part of the world of making books,
but she wanted to *write* books:

poems about running in a field of violets,
the beauty of a spider's web glistening with dew,
collecting fireflies and setting them free again,
the joy of splashing in puddles after a cool summer rain . . .

"The Violet. . . .
And yet it was a lovely flow'r,
Its colours bright and fair"

. . . and stars.
Always the stars.
Writing was her way to make everything brighter.

"I used to roam and revel 'mid the stars. . . .
When in my attic, with untold delight,
I watched the changing splendours of the night."

Jane polished her poems: each word, each line, each verse. Using pen names, both she and Ann sent their poems to publishers. Book publishers believed most people would not buy a book written by a woman, so women hid their real names behind pen names.

And Jane thought her words could shine as brightly on the page as any male poets' could.

But when Jane's poems came back to her, rejected, her hope faded.

Jane held in her sadness until she could secretly escape again,

to the stars,

to write and to believe

in poems . . . in stars . . . in herself.

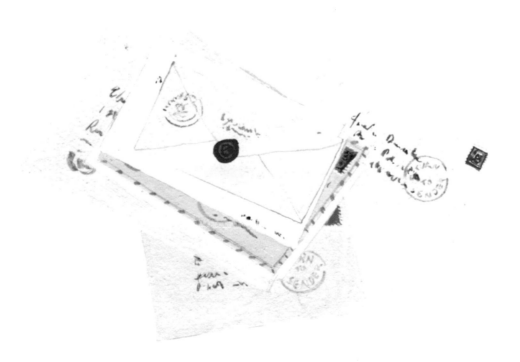

At last, both Jane and Ann had poems published in a small magazine for children. When a publisher read them, he asked to see more of their poems. Jane gathered together all her verses and rhymes, the poems of her life, like memories. Ann added her poems, and they sent them out into the world. The publisher bought them all and printed them in a book.

The Taylor sisters' book sold well all over England, but Jane was never one to boast of her success. She was concerned with only one thing: that children enjoyed reading her book.

Jane and Ann hoped that people reading their poems would feel what they experienced: running in the meadows, gazing at stars, a childhood of poetry.

Children loved how Jane's words sparkled, her verses shined, her poems were bright as stars.

Jane and Ann began working on another book. Jane set up a
writing room in the attic, with a view of the sky at night, to be as close
to the stars as possible. She wanted to write her best poems ever.

One evening, as a star twinkled in the sky, Jane thought she heard
the words, the *hush hush* of her mother's song, just as she did as a
child. Poetry and music blew together in the breeze.

She searched for the perfect words.

She wished and she wondered:

Could her poem be like a song?

She thought of reading and singing with her mother,

the nights gazing at stars with her father,

and all the stars she ever wished upon.

Jane hummed and felt the words' swirling rhythm soothe like a
lullaby and shimmer . . .

like a diamond in the sky.

This poem she titled "The Star."

She sent it in the collection, and the book was printed.

Jane and Ann now made a living entirely from their books. Ann married and stopped writing for many years, but Jane explored even more in her writing: poems for children and for adult readers too.

Then Jane published a novel for children. Because she wrote and sold books that children wanted to read, her publisher took a chance and put Jane's full name on the cover of the book.

When she saw her name in print, she felt like that tiny star in the sky, no longer struggling, but shining brightly at last.

Even when Jane was a busy and an accomplished author, poems still danced in her head, like they did when she was young. She wrote every morning after her walks in the country sun, and she wrote every night, always looking at the twinkling stars.

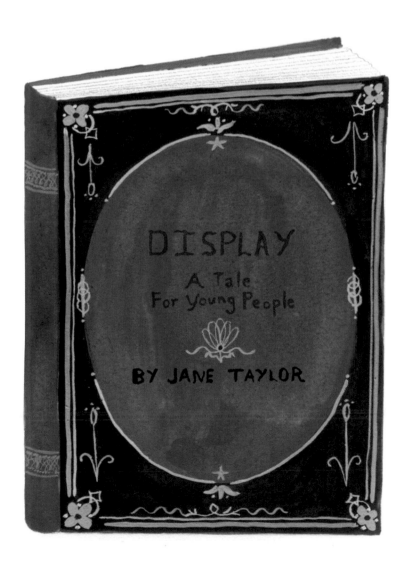

AUTHOR'S NOTE

Jane Taylor was one of England's most famous children's poets until her death in 1824. She helped to change children's literature forever. Her writing sparked a revolution in books for young people, which spread across England and then to America. Now girls and boys grow up loving books.

"The Star" remained children's favorite poem of all, shining the brightest among the poems of Jane's life. In 1838, a music publisher set the words to the tune of a famous French folk song, and Jane's poem became "Twinkle, Twinkle, Little Star." I bet you know it well!

Jane Taylor never heard her poem as a song, but stories and music, poems and songs passed down through time shine on.

Children everywhere keep dreaming and wishing under stars.

Hush, hush.

Hear them all singing?

DO STARS TWINKLE?

Modern astronomers now know that stars do not actually twinkle. Starlight bends as it travels toward us on Earth. Some of the light reaches our planet, but the rest bends slightly away from us. When we look at stars from our place on Earth, it is due to the atmosphere, temperatures, and air density that they seem to glisten and sparkle.

JANE TAYLOR, 1783–1824

Jane Taylor was born in London on September 23, 1783. The Taylors moved to Suffolk when Jane was three to save money and live in the quiet of the countryside, and then to Colchester when she was thirteen. Her parents taught both Jane and her sister, Ann, at home, schooling them in subjects like astronomy, anatomy, literature, mechanics, geography, geometry, and history. Jane's favorite things were writing, poetry, and astronomy. Jane would often spend time outdoors at night with her father, gazing at and studying the stars. It is most likely that the roots of "The Star" came from recollections of Jane's youngest days in Suffolk, where it was said the sky was exceptionally clear, like a dome of twinkling stars. Most of Jane's poems for children focus on the childhood delights of living in the country, on nature, and on animals.

Jane's parents wanted her to learn the family engraving trade because they knew publishing would be difficult for a woman, and Jane's mother feared her daughter being called a "bluestocking." But Jane was determined and brave. At night, after working long hours engraving, Jane wrote in her attic room with a large window's view of the sky and meadows. This is where Jane wrote her most famous poem, "The Star," which launched her career as a children's poet and writer.

"The Star" is a typical poem from the Romantic era (circa 1790–1850), when poets tried to capture the beauty of nature in simple language. Jane hoped to inspire young children's imaginations through her poetry. Her works were among the first of their kind written for children's enjoyment rather than for purely educational purposes.

Poetry was held in the highest regard during Jane Taylor's time, and even male poets often signed with pen names or initials to maintain the notion of their poetry as lofty and the most respected form of literature. Some scholars and sources differ in their research on this topic, but there is no doubt that women writers of the Romantic era struggled in the shadow of male writers. But the perseverance of women like Jane blazed the path to the acceptance of women as writers in the nineteenth century and beyond. Both Jane and Ann made a profitable living from their books.

When *Original Poems, for Infant Minds* was published in 1804, the publishers did not identify any of the authors by name. *Rhymes for the Nursery* came out in 1806. On that cover, Jane and her sister remained anonymous, with only "Written by the authors of *Original Poems, for Infant Minds*" as their credit. Jane and her sister, Ann, had several pen names throughout their lives, including "Several Young Persons," "Q.Q.," and "Authors of *Original Poems*." It was not until 1815 and her children's novel, *Display: A Tale for Young People*, that Jane Taylor's full name appeared on the cover of any of her works.

Despite the odds against her as a woman, Jane was a prolific poet and writer. She died on April 13, 1824, at age forty of breast cancer. Before her death, Jane said that her mind was "still teeming with unfulfilled projects."

QUOTES AND SOURCES

"contemplate the dark blue depths of the sky"

The Writings of Jane Taylor in Five Volumes, Isaac Taylor, ed., vol. I, *Memoirs and Poetical Remains* (Boston: Perkins and Marvin, 1832), 132–133.

"safe, certain, and secure a means to independence"

The Writings of Jane Taylor in Five Volumes, Isaac Taylor, ed., vol. I, *Memoirs and Poetical Remains* (Boston: Perkins and Marvin, 1832), 55.

"The Violet. . . . And yet it was a lovely flow'r, Its colours bright and fair"

Jane Taylor and Ann Taylor, "The Violet," *Original Poems, for Infant Minds* (Philadelphia: T. Ash, 1834), 164.

"The spider is weaving her delicate thread, which brilliantly glitters with dew"

Jane Taylor, Miss (Adelaide) O'Keeffe, and Ann Taylor, "Morning," *Original Poems, for Infant Minds* (Philadelphia: Frankish, 1821), 26.

"I used to roam and revel 'mid the stars. . . . When in my attic, with untold delight, I watched the changing splendours of the night."

The Writings of Jane Taylor in Five Volumes, Isaac Taylor, ed., vol. I, *Memoirs and Poetical Remains* (Boston: Perkins and Marvin, 1832), 42.

"like a diamond in the sky"

Jane Taylor and Ann Taylor, "The Star," *Rhymes for the Nursery* (London: Darnton and Harvey, 1806), 10–11.

"Twinkle, twinkle, little star,/How I wonder what you are!/Up above the world so high./ Like a diamond in the sky. Twinkle, twinkle, little star. How I wonder what you are."

W. E. Hickson, *The Singing Master* (London: Taylor and Walton, 1840), 100–101.

"still teeming with unfulfilled projects"

"Jane Taylor, Biography," Poem Hunter. Accessed January 27, 2021. https://www.poemhunter.com/jane-taylor/biography/.

"The Star"

Jane Taylor and Ann Taylor, *Rhymes for the Nursery* (London: Darnton and Harvey, 1806), 10–11.

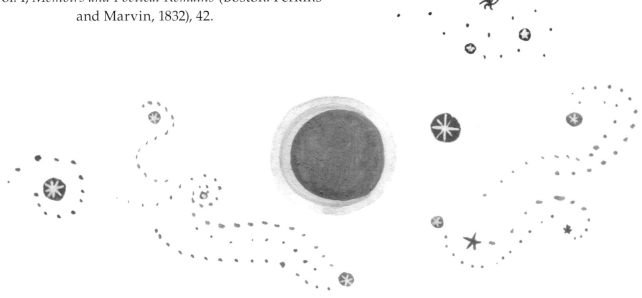

TIMELINE OF SELECTED WORKS
BY JANE TAYLOR

1803   Jane's poem "The Beggar Boy" is accepted for publication by William Darnton.

1804   "The Beggar Boy" is published in *Minor's Pocket Book.*

1804   Darnton and Harvey in London published *Original Poems, for Infant Minds,* by Several Young Persons (poems by Jane Taylor and Ann Taylor as well as poems by Adelaide O'Keeffe, Isaac Taylor Jr., and Bernard Barton).

1805   Multiple works for children and young people (collaborations with Ann, Isaac Taylor Jr., and the Reverend Isaac Taylor), including: *Rural Scenes: or, A Peep into the Country for Good Children* (1805); *Limed Twigs, to Catch Young Birds* (1808); *The New Cries of London* (1808); *Signor Topsy-Turvey's Wonderful Magic Lantern; or, The World Turned Upside Down* (1810); *The Mother's Fables, in Verse. Designed Through the Medium of Amusement, to Correct Some of the Faults and Follies of Children* (1812); and many more works and books throughout her life.

1806   Darnton and Harvey publish *Rhymes for the Nursery,* "Written by the authors of *Original Poems, for Infant Minds*" (poems by Jane and Ann Taylor only).

1810   *Hymns for Infant Minds* (by Jane, Ann, and Isaac Taylor Jr.).

1815   *Display: A Tale for Young People* (first work of Jane Taylor's published with her full and real name on the title page).

1816   *Essays in Rhyme on Morals and Manners* (for adult readers).

1817   Jane collaborated with her mother on *Correspondence Between a Mother and Her Daughter at School.*

1824   *The Contributions of Q.Q. to a Periodical Work* (published posthumously).

1825   *Memoirs and Poetical Remains of the Late Jane Taylor; with Extracts from Her Correspondence,* Isaac Taylor, ed., 2 vols.

1838   "The Star" is published as a song, "Twinkle, Twinkle, Little Star," in *The Singing Master,* a collection of popular children's songs by W. E. Hickson.

1849   *The Little Wanderer* (published posthumously, Ann Taylor stated this was Jane Taylor's work).

1867   *The Family Pen. Memorials, Biographical and Literary, of the Taylor Family, of Ongar,* Rev. Isaac Taylor, ed. [with selections from the works of Isaac Taylor Sr., Jane Taylor, Jefferys Taylor, and Ann Taylor], 2 vols.

BIBLIOGRAPHY

PRIMARY

Bouin, François, and Joseph Renou. *Les Amusements D'une Heure Et Demy Ou Les Jolis Airs Variés Contenant Six Divertissements Champêtres Pour Violons, Flûtes, Hautbois, Pardessus De Violles Ou Musettes.* Fourth ed. Gravé. Paris: privately published, 1762.

Hickson, W. E. *The Singing Master.* London: Taylor and Walton, 1838.

Hickson, W. E. *The Singing Master.* London: Taylor and Walton, 1840.

Taylor, Ann. *Autobiography and Other Memorials of Mrs. Gilbert, (Formerly Ann Taylor).* Edited by Josiah Gilbert. London: H.S. King, 1874.

Taylor, Isaac, ed. *Memoirs, Correspondence, and Poetical Remains of Jane Taylor.* London, England: Holdsworth and Ball, 1831.

Taylor, Isaac, ed. *The Writings of Jane Taylor in Five Volumes.* Vol. I, *Memoirs and Poetical Remains.* Boston: Perkins and Marvin, 1832. https://digital.library.upenn.edu/women/taylor/memoirs/memoirs.html.

Taylor, Jane, and Ann Taylor. "The Star." *Rhymes for the Nursery.* London: Darnton and Harvey, 1806. https://www.bl.uk/collection-items/first-publication-of-twinkle-twinkle-little-star.

Taylor, Jane, Miss (Adelaide) O'Keeffe, and Ann Taylor. *Original Poems, for Infant Minds.* Philadelphia: Frankish, 1821.

Taylor, Jane, and Ann Taylor. *Original Poems, for Infant Minds.* Philadelphia: T. Ash, 1834.

Taylor, Jane, and Ann Taylor. *Rhymes for the Nursery.* New York: D. Appleton, 1849.

SECONDARY

Balfour, Clara Lucas. *Women Worth Emulating.* New York: American Tract Society, 1877.

"The Childhood of Jane Taylor." *Parley's Magazine* 9: (1841): 293–302. New York: C.S. Francis, 1841.

Cryer, Max. *Love Me Tender: The Stories behind the World's Best-loved Songs.* London: Frances Lincoln, 2008.

Feldman, Paula R., ed. *British Women Poets of the Romantic Era: An Anthology.* Baltimore, MD: Johns Hopkins University Press, 1997.

Feldman, Paula R. "Women Poets and Anonymity in the Romantic Era." *New Literary History* 33.2 (2002): 279–89. Accessed July 8, 2017. https://scholarcommons.sc.edu/cgi/viewcontent.cgi?article=1257&context=engl_facpub.

Hill, Mildred J., and Patty Smith Hill. *Song Stories for the Kindergarten.* Chicago: Clayton F. Summy Co., 1896.

Jackson, J. R. de J., ed. *Romantic Poetry by Women: A Bibliography 1770–1835.* Oxford: Clarendon Press, 1993.

Knight, Helen Cross. "Jane Taylor: Her Life and Letters." *The Taylors of Ongar and Others of Their Family.* T. Nelson and Sons, 1880. Accessed July 8, 2017. https://archive.org/details/janetaylorherli00kniggoog.

Morton, Timothy. "Twinkle Twinkle Little Star as an Ambient Poem; a Study of a Dialectical Image, with Some Remarks on Coleridge and Wordsworth." *Romantic Circles.* University of Maryland, 2001. Accessed Aug. 21, 2014. https://romantic-circles.org/praxis/ecology/morton/morton.html.